KING CUDGEL'S
CHALLENGE

Sch

KING CUDGEL'S CHALLENGE

Karen Wallace

illustrated by Helen Flook

A & C Black • London

First published 2006 by
A & C Black Publishers Ltd
38 Soho Square, London, W1D 3HB

www.acblack.com

ISBN 0-7136-7553-5
ISBN 978-0-7136-7553-5

A CIP catalogue for this book is available from the British Library.

Chapter One

King Cudgel screamed and screamed. The sound that came out was somewhere between a squeak and a whimper.

A mouse pushed its furry face through a patch of grass. 'What's your problem?' it demanded angrily.

King Cudgel stared into a pair of hard beady eyes and realised to his horror that he was the same size as the mouse! No wonder he sounded so squeaky! No wonder no one had heard him calling! He clambered onto a stone and shouted:

'I am King Cudgel of Crunchbone Castle! Ruler of this kingdom! Help! Help!'

Suddenly the ground shook, and two voices the king knew so well filled the air. The sound was like a giant's fingernails scraping across a blackboard.

'It's *my* kingdom!' screamed Prince Marvin.

'No, it's *mine*!' yelled Princess Gusty Ox.

King Cudgel froze with horror. Any minute now, his children would crush him underfoot. And they wouldn't even notice! Worst of all, they wouldn't even care.

King Cudgel jumped down from his stone.

'Please! Please!' he begged the mouse, who was still staring at him. 'Can I hide in your nest? It's my children, you see. They'll—'

'Will you promise to stop squeaking?' interrupted the mouse.

'Promise,' whimpered King Cudgel.

The ground shook. The terrible shouting grew louder.

The mouse pointed up to a ball of woven straw attached to the long stiff grass. 'Help yourself!' it said.

King Cudgel ran as fast as his tiny legs would carry him. He climbed up the stalk and curled up in the mouse's nest. A second later, the prince and princess thundered past, hitting each other with sticks and roaring like tigers.

The king's trusty servant looked at the ball of sheets that quivered on the royal four-poster bed. 'Your Majesty!' said Quail, in his calmest voice. 'Your Majesty! Wake up! You're just having a bad dream.'

King Cudgel's spaniel, Fluffy, whined and pawed at the twisted pillowcases. Quail gently pulled at a corner of the curtain.

'A dream?' cried King Cudgel. He poked his nose above the bedclothes. 'It's a *nightmare*, Quail!' he said. 'And I have it *every* night!'

The king fell back on the pillows. 'If I didn't have Fluffy to comfort me—' He closed his eyes.

'Is your nightmare about the Prince Marvin and the Princess Gusty Ox by any chance?' asked Quail. He stirred ten sugars into the king's morning mug of tea and put it down beside the royal bed.

King Cudgel opened his eyes and sat up. He grasped the mug in both hands and began to slurp noisily.

'What am I going to do, Quail?' he said. 'Prince Marvin has never shared anything in his life and Princess Gusty Ox wants everything for herself.'

He scooped out the sugar from the bottom of the cup with his finger and stuck it in his mouth. 'I thought twins were supposed to get on. Why do mine fight all the time?'

'You should never have told them you wanted to give up your kingdom and move to the seaside,' replied Quail. He squeezed out a damp cloth and wiped the king's fingers before everything in the room was covered with sticky marks. 'It's only made things worse.'

King Cudgel groaned. It was his dream to retire to a place of his own overlooking the sea. He'd thought about it for ages and finally come up with the perfect name: *Seaview.*

His eyes travelled across the room to a portrait of his wife. She was an enormous woman with a face like a battle-axe and arms like sides of bacon. One day, she had picked up a walking stick instead of her sword and gone out bear hunting. She had never returned.

'I wish Lady Carrion were here,' King Cudgel sighed. 'She's the only one who can stop the children fighting because she shouts louder than they do.'

Quail looked at the portrait and immediately his hands began to shake. Queen Carrion had been famous for two things: her collection of bear skins and her terrible temper. Crackle, the court wizard, once declared that he'd seen the air turn purple because of her swear words.

King Cudgel grabbed a handful of sugar lumps from his emergency bedside casket, and shoved them in his mouth.

'How can I retire when my children can't even share a bar of chocolate without tearing each other to bits?' he wailed suddenly.

From the open window came a loud ripping sound, then a *crack* as if someone had hit someone else over the head with a stick.

'The kingdom's *mine*,' screamed the voice of Princess Gusty Ox.

'No, it's *mine*,' snarled the voice of Prince Marvin.

'Stink brain!'

'Elephant legs!'

There was a *splash* as something, or *someone*, was thrown in the moat. A second later, Prince Marvin squealed like a stuck pig.

Quail shut the windows and drew the curtains again. It was the best he could do to block out the noise. If only some witch would come along and turn the children into stone, like they used to do in the old days. That would stop them fighting!

Quail gasped. Why hadn't he thought of it before? King Cudgel didn't have a witch but he did have a *wizard*!

'I've got it, sire!' he cried. 'Ask Crackle what to do! It's about time he worked for a living. All he does is sun himself.'

King Cudgel leapt out of bed. 'What a brilliant idea!' he shouted with delight. 'Crackle shall cast a spell to make my children stop fighting! Then they will share the kingdom and I can retire to the seaside!'

Quail bowed and smiled proudly. 'Shall I put out our favourite leopard-skin leggings and the doublet edged in purple feathers?' he asked. For despite his problems, the king was always a flashy dresser.

'Yes indeed,' cried King Cudgel. 'Then summon Crackle! We'll settle this once and for all!'

Chapter Two

Princess Gusty Ox stomped around the forest, breaking tree trunks with both hands. It was something she did every morning to keep her arm muscles strong. Princess Gusty Ox liked to keep fit, and one day, she would be Queen of Crunchbone Castle, so she had to be tough to fight off intruders.

Especially intruders like her brother, stink-brain Prince Marvin.

Suddenly the ground gave away beneath her great boots and she tumbled into a hole. The next minute, a nasty laugh floated above her and the air was filled with something that smelled like ferret sweat.

'Got you!' cried Prince Marvin from the edge of the hole. 'Now I'm going drop a snake on your head!' He grinned down at her and ran a skinny hand through his fine blonde hair. 'Unless you promise to give me your share of the kingdom!'

19

'No way,' muttered his sister. 'You're nothing but a weedy stink brain. You can't even lift a battle-axe! You could never be king.'

'Just because I don't have legs like an elephant and arms like a wrestler,' snarled Prince Marvin. He dangled the snake in the air. 'Now, what's it going to be? Do I get the whole kingdom, or not?'

'You'd never have the guts to pick up a *real* snake,' said Princess Gusty Ox, ignoring his question. 'That's only a rubber one!'

'Wrong again, elephant legs!' cried Prince Marvin. He dropped the snake and ran away as fast as he could.

Princess Gusty Ox let out a howl of fury. She hated snakes! With one great heave, she was out of the hole and running after her brother, waving a big, fat stick.

As usual, Crackle, the court wizard, had turned himself into a frog. He was in the moat, sunning his belly on a lily pad, when Prince Marvin ran past.

Prince Marvin liked hurting things, especially small creatures. He picked up a stone and threw it, hard. 'Take that, you stupid frog!' he yelled.

The stone hit Crackle on his froggy face and he hopped quickly out of the water.

A second later, Princess Gusty Ox thumped past. Frogs were as bad as snakes in her book. She kicked out with her size-eleven boot.

Crackle moved quickly, but not quickly enough. The princess caught his leg and knocked him back into the water.

At that moment, Quail appeared. Quick as a flash, Crackle turned himself back into a wizard and clambered out of the moat with as much dignity as he could manage.

'There you are!' cried Quail. 'I've been looking for you everywhere.' He peered at the wizard's face. 'That's a terrible black eye you've got.'

'Like the bruise on my leg,' muttered Crackle.

'Sunning yourself on a lily pad again?' replied Quail knowingly. 'I warned you about that.'

'Those children—' Crackle rubbed his eye. 'One day I'll sort them out, I swear it.'

Quail took Crackle's arm. He helped the wizard as he hobbled painfully across the grass to the castle gates. 'You might get the chance sooner than you think,' he said. 'The king has a job for you!'

∞

King Cudgel looked at the rusty kettle. It didn't look magic to him. 'Are you sure this is going to work?' he asked.

'Of course it will, sire,' replied Crackle, trying not to sound cross. He filled the kettle with water and hung it over a small fire. 'Just you wait and see!'

A few minutes later, steam poured out of the kettle's spout and the king watched as Crackle waved his magic wand and said something that sounded very like *abracadabra*!

Suddenly the steam formed a square. 'Ah ha!' cried Crackle. 'The magic window into the future.' He peered into the square and a great grin spread across his face.

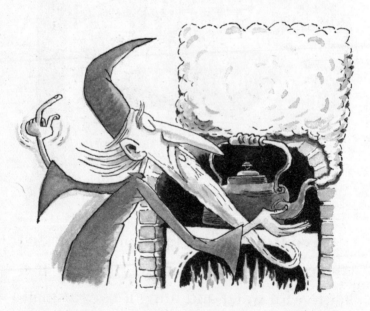

King Cudgel looked over his shoulder.

'What is it? I can't see anything,' he said in a bad-tempered voice.

King Cudgel hated being left out.

'Of course you can't, sire,' replied Crackle. '*You're* not a wizard!'

'So what is it?' asked Quail quickly, before the king went into one of his famous sulks.

'The solution!' announced Crackle, proudly. 'Sire, your nightmares are over!'

'Quail!' cried King Cudgel. 'Summon Prince Marvin and Princess Gusty Ox! Tell them their kingdom is at stake!' Then he turned to Crackle. 'Now, what *exactly* did you see…'

Princess Gusty Ox had Prince Marvin pinned to the ground. She was just about to jump on him, when Quail rushed out of the castle door.

'Stop that immediately and come with me,' he ordered. 'Your kingdom is at stake!'

The princess turned and waved a sharpened stick in Quail's face. 'Get lost, Tremblehead,' she snarled. 'The only stake that matters is this one, and it's about to go through my brother.'

'Princess Gusty Ox,' said Quail. 'Your father commands your presence. Unless you do as I say, you and Prince Marvin will lose your right to the kingdom!'

The princess dropped the stick and climbed reluctantly off her brother. 'If you're having me on, Twitchwobble, I'll—'

'Oh shuddup, elephant legs,' muttered Prince Marvin. 'It's my kingdom, anyway.'

'No, it's not.'

'Yes, it is.'

'No.'

'Yes.'

'No.'

It was unbearable. Quail put his fingers in his ears. 'Follow me,' he said, then he walked quickly back to the castle door.

Chapter Three

'I ain't accepting no challenge!' snorted
Princess Gusty Ox. She turned to Crackle.
'I don't care what that black-eyed creep
saw in his steam square.'

'It's not fair,' whined Prince Marvin.
'Anyway, challenges are dumb.'

Crackle had been expecting this to happen. He had advised the king to dress in his most important-looking clothes and wear the biggest, spikiest crown he could find.

Now, King Cudgel stood up and held out his arms. In his enormous cloak, he looked a cross between a giant, gold bat and a skinny, red turkey with a beak like a parsnip.

'You will do as you're told!' he bellowed. Then he looked into his children's faces for as long he could before he began to feel sick. 'If you don't accept my challenge, your cousin, Godric the Geek, will take over the kingdom when I retire!'

Princess Gusty Ox and Prince Marvin stared at each other in horror. Godric the Geek was the wettest twit ever. He knitted his own stockings. He liked arranging flowers. He even changed his tunic without being asked. The idea of Godric the Geek telling them what to do was absolutely awful. For a moment the great chamber was completely silent. You could have heard a goblin cough.

Princess Gusty Ox scuffed her boot back and forth across the stone floor. Prince Marvin chewed a lock of his hair and pulled at a loose thread in his sleeve.

'What do we have to do then?' asked Princess Gusty Ox at last.

'Over to you, Crackle,' said the king.

It was Crackle's great moment! He leapt into the middle of the chamber and waved his wand in the air. Sparks flew out of his pointy hat and a triumphant grin split his face.

'This is the challenge!' he cried. 'First you must find the golden pack of cards! Next you must play the *right* game! Only then will you learn the secret that will keep you the kingdom! You have three days to complete the task and you must stay *together* all the time!'

Princess Gusty Ox and Prince Marvin looked at each other. Even though they hated one another's guts, they were agreed on this: *anything* was better than having Godric the Geek rule the kingdom.

The princess glared at Crackle. 'OK, you frog-faced clown,' she muttered. 'When do we start?'

∞

No one came to say goodbye to Princess Gusty Ox and Prince Marvin. They were too busy celebrating.

The idea that the castle would be peaceful for three whole days was too good to be true.

The royal children went down to the kitchen, where Quail had left them sandwiches for the first day. There was a note in Crackle's writing: *After this, you're on your own.*

∞

Princess Gusty Ox trudged down a path in the forest, her great boots sending shock waves through the ground.

At first she decided to ignore Crackle's orders and stayed as far away from Prince Marvin as possible. Apart from anything else, she knew he had already eaten all his sandwiches and would try to steal hers the moment she wasn't looking. Then she realised that if she lost him, they would lose the challenge and Godric the Geek would get the kingdom.

Suddenly Prince Marvin dropped from an overhanging branch and landed on her shoulders.

'This is all your fault!' he screamed.

'No, it's not!'

'Yes, it is.'

'No.'

'Yes.'

'No.'

At once the forest went dark and a great light appeared in the sky. Princess Gusty Ox and Prince Marvin looked up and their hearts froze.

A picture of Godric the Geek hung above them, as if painted with stars. He was wearing the spiky Crunchbone crown and there was a nasty smirk on his face.

Without a word, Prince Marvin slid off his sister's back and they carried on walking into the forest, side by side.

'It's too deep!' screamed Prince Marvin, standing on a bank and looking out over a scummy, stinky river. 'I can't swim!'

'Then how are you going to get across, stink brain?' asked Princess Gusty Ox.

'I'm not, elephant legs!' snarled Prince Marvin. 'I'm going home!'

'You can't!' yelled Princess Gusty Ox. 'You heard what Crackle said. We've got to do this *together*.'

'Then you'll have to carry me!' Prince Marvin glared at his sister.

'No way!'

In front of them, the water stirred. Something strange was happening in the scum. Bits of green weed swirled into a picture. Godric the Geek appeared and this time his smirk was even bigger.

The princess bent down so that her brother could climb onto her shoulders. 'All right,' she muttered. 'But I still hate you.'

On the other side of the river, the ground was soft and swampy.

'There are no cards here,' whined Prince Marvin.

'Maybe they're in a golden box which has sunk in the mud,' said Princess Gusty Ox. She bent down on her hands and knees and started to feel around in the stinking slime.

Even though he felt sick, Prince Marvin bent down and did the same. He couldn't bear the idea that she might find the pack of cards before him.

All that day, the prince and princess crawled through the smelly mud feeling for something hard and square. Mosquitoes bit them. Flies tickled their noses. Beetles crawled under their tunics and made them itch and scratch.

At the end of the day, they heaved themselves out of the swamp and sat down against a wall. They were both too tired to wash the mud from their clothes and they were too tired to fight over who smelled worst. They closed their eyes and fell asleep.

∞

The next day they came to a field full of flat stones.

'Do you think the cards are under one of these stones?' asked Princess Gusty Ox.

'How should I know, elephant legs?' replied Prince Marvin. He picked up a stone and threw it at his sister's head.

Princess Gusty Ox rolled a large boulder towards her brother. 'Sissy, stink brain!' she said when he yelped and jumped to one side.

A huge swarm of wasps appeared in the sky like a black cloud. The prince and princess threw themselves on the ground and wrapped their arms around their heads. Then, peering through their fingers, they saw a truly terrible sight. The wasps had formed the shape of Godric the Geek and the smirk on his face was wider than ever.

Prince Marvin got up and began to turn over stones as fast as possible. Instantly, Princess Gusty Ox was on her feet, too. But no matter how many stones they turned over, they found nothing.

At the end of the day, their fingers were cut and blistered and their nails were torn. They slumped down by the trunk of a tall tree. They were too worn out and hungry to keep looking. They were even too tired to fight.

'It's no good,' sighed Princess Gusty Ox. 'We're going to lose the challenge.'

'Mabye that's what Father planned,' muttered Prince Marvin. 'Maybe he really wants Godric the Geek to rule the kingdom.'

'I think you're right.' Princess Gusty Ox picked her teeth with a twig. 'He hardly ever talks to us, does he?'

'Probably because he can't get a word in edgeways.' Prince Marvin was about to laugh. Then, for the first time ever, he thought what he'd said might not be funny. So he chewed his lip instead.

At that moment a squirrel appeared from a hole in the tree above them. Prince Marvin picked up a stone. It was a sharp one and he was a good shot. He raised his arm and took aim.

To the prince's surprise, the squirrel cocked his head and didn't move. It had a funny look in its eye and reminded him of someone, but he couldn't think who.

Again Prince Marvin did something he had never done before. He dropped the stone and watched the squirrel scamper back along the branch.

Princess Gusty Ox opened her mouth to call him a sissy stink brain, then she closed it again. She'd noticed the look in the squirrel's eye, too, and was glad that her brother hadn't hurt it.

The next moment something amazing happened. A pack of cards fell out of the hole where the squirrel had been. And, as it tumbled down through the branches, flashes of gold sparkled on the forest floor!

Chapter Four

It was the final day of the challenge and nothing was going right. No matter how hard Princess Gusty Ox and Prince Marvin tried not to fight, they just couldn't stop themselves.

So every game they played ended up in an argument.

First it was about card castles.

Prince Marvin said Princess Gusty Ox's castle didn't count because it was too wide at the bottom. Princess Gusty Ox said Prince Marvin's was no good because he used pine-cone glue to stick his cards together.

Then they tried playing poker and used acorns to bet with, but that didn't work either because they both cheated too much.

'How are we going to find the *right* game?' wailed Princess Gusty Ox.

Prince Marvin only rolled on his back and kicked the air with his feet.

What's wrong with you?' cried Princess Gusty Ox.

'I'm *starving!*' wailed Prince Marvin. 'I haven't eaten for *days!*'

Princess Gusty Ox put her hand inside her pocket. In it were some berries she had picked off a bush when her brother wasn't looking. Suddenly it occurred to her that if they were going to win the challenge, they would have to help each other. She handed the berries to him.

Prince Marvin stopped rolling immediately. 'You sure?' he muttered, barely able to meet his sister's eye.

Princess Gusty Ox nodded.

Prince Marvin was just about to swallow the handful in one gulp, when he changed his mind and gave some back to his sister. She must be just as hungry as he was.

The prince and princess stared at each other. They knew they were both thinking the same thing: *Why did they fight all the time?* It wasn't just about the kingdom. They'd fought since they were old enough to pick up a stick.

'I wonder if all brothers and sisters are like us,' said Princess Gusty Ox.

'Dunno,' replied Prince Marvin. He chewed his lip. 'Father might know but, like you said, he never talks to us.'

'I don't think he likes us much,' said Princess Gusty Ox.

Prince Marvin scratched the ground with his fingers. 'We're not very nice to him, are we?' he said.

'No,' mumbled Princess Gusty Ox.

A gust of wind swirled around the bottom of the tree and tossed the cards in the air.

Princess Gusty Ox and Prince Marvin looked down. They both saw two Queens facing up. 'SNAP!' they shouted at the same time, and burst out laughing.

Suddenly the sun was brighter, the sky was bluer and birds started to sing. The royal children picked up the cards and began to play.

'Snap!'

'Snap!'

'Snap!'

'Snap!'

It was the first time they had ever really enjoyed a game together. So they played again … and again … and again. In fact, they were having such a good time, they didn't notice that the sun was sinking in the sky.

'Marv!' cried Princess Gusty Ox. She'd promised never to call her brother stink brain again.

Prince Marvin looked up from his stack of cards and grinned. 'What is it, Big G?' In return, he'd promised to stop calling his sister elephant legs.

Princess Gusty Ox grinned from ear to ear. 'I think we've found the *right* game!'

Prince Marvin grinned back. 'Me, too! Let's go home!'

'Jump on my shoulders!' cried Princess Gusty Ox. 'It's the fastest way!' And they set off through the forest.

Chapter Five

King Cudgel woke up to the most extraordinary noise. At first, he didn't know what it was. Sometimes it sounded like chuckling water. Sometimes it sounded like a pigeon cooing or a rooster crowing.

The king moaned and pulled a pillow over his head. Of course he knew it was impossible but it almost sounded like children's laughter.

'Wakey! Wakey!' Quail skipped into the room balancing a tea tray on his head.

King Cudgel poked his nose over the sheets. 'What's that noise?' he said.

Quail put down the tray, drew back the curtains and opened the window. The noise was louder than ever.

'The Princess Gusty Ox and the Prince Marvin have returned, sire!' cried Quail. 'Look! I've never seen anything like it!'

King Cudgel slid out of bed. He walked over to the window and peered outside. He grabbed a table to stop himself from fainting. His children were playing on a seesaw!

'When did they get back?' croaked King Cudgel.

'Early this morning, sire. They didn't want to disturb you.'

King Cudgel felt a wave of dizziness wash over him. It was the first time his children had ever thought of anyone except themselves.

'Summon Crackle!' he cried. 'He'll know what this means.'

'Crackle has been summoned, sire,' said Quail proudly. 'I took the liberty myself.'

As he spoke, he opened the king's wardrobe and took out a pair of stripey velvet pantaloons and an open-necked shirt embroidered with comets.

Then he put a pair of pointed, purple shoes with diamond buckles on the floor. It was King Cudgel's party outfit and Quail was certain there would be something to celebrate that day.

A moment later, Crackle floated into the room. He was so pleased with himself, he couldn't make his feet touch the ground.

'Crackle!' cried King Cudgel. He was looking outside again. Now Princess Gusty Ox and Prince Marvin were playing ping pong on the castle green. 'What does this mean?'

'It means the steam never lies,' replied Crackle, barely able to hide the triumph in his voice. 'It means that your dear children have completed their challenge and learned a very important lesson. It means that now you can retire to the seaside.'

'But what have they learned?' asked King Cudgel. Happy voices rang out from the courtyard below. 'I don't understand.'

'They have learned to get on with each other,' explained Crackle. 'They have learned that fighting is a waste of time.'

'And not nice for anyone,' added Quail.

'And not nice at all,' agreed Crackle.

King Cudgel could barely believe what he was hearing. 'How long will it last?' he asked.

'For ever,' replied Crackle. 'Sire, as I predicted, your nightmares are now over.' He bowed and waved his cape. 'Now, if you'll excuse me, after all this hard work, I'm going to sun my belly on a lily pad.'

The king waved him away and Crackle floated back through the open door. The room went silent. King Cudgel went and sat down on the edge of his bed.

He opened his emergency bedside casket and filled his mouth with sugar lumps. 'Quail,' he said in a trembling voice. 'I don't know what to do.'

Quail frowned. 'What is wrong, sire?'

Princess Gusty Ox's voice rose through the air:

'Great serve, Marv!'

'Fab rally, Big G!'

They laughed and the sharp *tap tap* of the ping-pong ball started up again.

King Cudgel groaned and held his head.

'I never believed they would ever stop fighting,' he said. 'That's why I wanted to retire to the seaside.'

'I guessed as much,' said Quail. 'And now you would like to change your mind?'

King Cudgel looked up and his eyes were bright. 'Do you think I could, Quail? I mean, it's not too late, is it?'

'You are the king, sire,' replied Quail. 'You can do what you want.' He picked up the party clothes and began to lay them out over the end of the bed.

'And I think you'll find that the prince and princess will be very happy if you stay here, too.'

King Cudgel walked over to the window. Beyond the castle walls, the meadows were full of wild flowers. Beyond the meadows, the hills were as green as emeralds and the forest was alive with birdsong. Crunchbone Castle was the loveliest place in the world.

Fluffy ran to the door barking as Princess Gusty Ox and Prince Marvin walked into the room.

King Cudgel couldn't believe it. Their eyes were shining, their cheeks were pink, but best of all were the smiles that spread over their faces.

'Congratulations!' cried King Cudgel. 'I'm very, very proud of you!'

Even Quail had to wipe a tear from his eye as Princess Gusty Ox and Prince Marvin ran into their father's arms.

King Cudgel hugged his children as hard as he could. 'We're going to be a proper family and live happily every after from now on,' he whispered. He gave them both an extra squeeze. 'And just so you know, I think Godric the Geek is the wettest twit in the kingdom, too!'